Lion Lullaby

Kate Banks

illustrated by Lauren Tobia

CANDLEWICK PRESS

First edition 2021

Library of Congress Catalog Card Number pending
ISBN 978-1-5362-0982-2

21 22 23 24 25 26 CCP 10 9 8 7 6 5 4 3 2 1

Printed in Shenzhen, Guangdong, China

This book was typeset in Cheltenham.
The illustrations were done in pencil and assembled digitally.

Candlewick Press
99 Dover Street
Somerville, Massachusetts 02144

www.candlewick.com

For Peter Anton and Max

KB

To Buwenda Pre-School and all at Soft Power Education

LT

Dusk paints stripes across the sky.

The moon is ripe and round.

Little lions everywhere listen to evening's sounds.

The wind is crying.

Trees are sighing.

It's time to run along home.

One little lion perched in a tree.

Where is it looking and what does it see?

A monkey is bouncing a babe on its knee.

Oh, little lion, hurry on home.

Two little lions crouched in the bush,
watching a cobra wiggle and slink
and wave its tail to the jackal's wail.

The zebras bray and the tree frog peeps.
Oh, little lions, it's time to sleep.

Three little lions sprint across the sand,
braving the dunes washed into waves.
The quiet is strumming.
Nightfall is coming.
Oh, little lions, run along home.

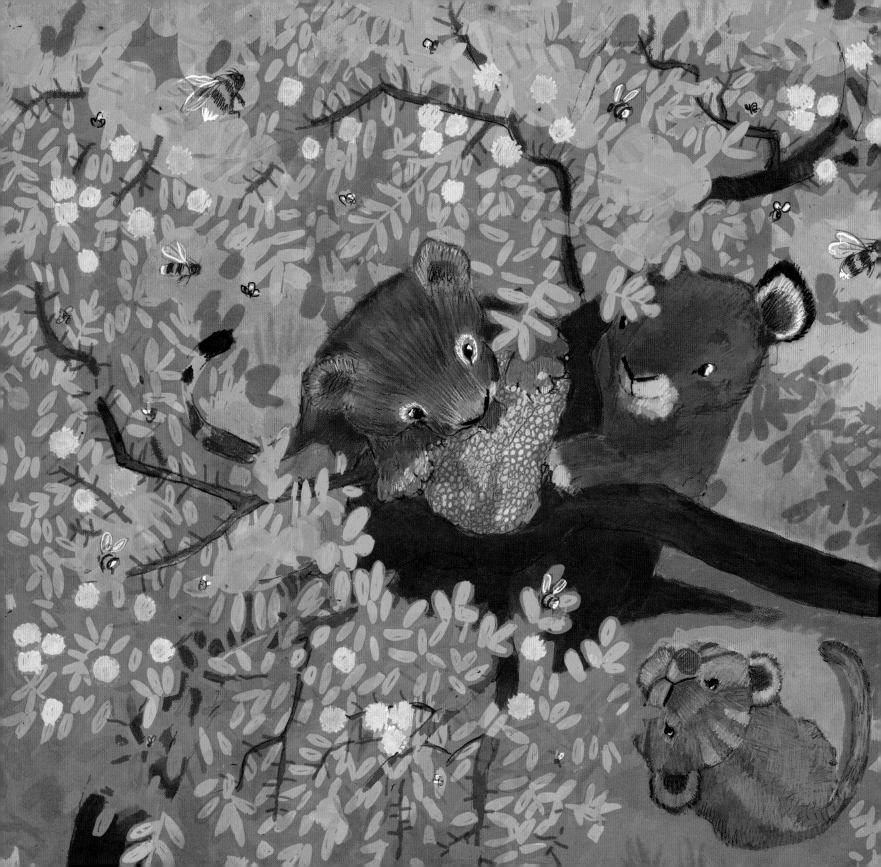

Four little lions on the prowl.
A buzzing blends with a faraway growl.

Someone is waiting to put you to bed.
Oh, little lions, hurry on home.

Five little lions crossing the stream,
nodding their heads and starting to dream.

The crickets are playing. Treetops are swaying.
Oh, little lions, come along home.

Six little lions climbing a hill.
Why is it trembling rather than still?

A pair of elephants are stomping their feet
while a herd of wildebeests drums a beat.
Oh, little lions, run along home.

Seven little lions caught in the rain,
walking through worlds where light becomes dim,
where loud becomes soft and out becomes in.
Oh, little lions, hurry on home.

Eight tired lions stopping to rest.
Rubbing their heads, licking their fur,
stretching their legs, starting to purr.

The door to dreamland opens wide.

"Come," sighs the wind, "and I'll take you inside."

Oh, little lions, it's time to come home.

Nine little lions roll in the grass.
How do they feel to be home at last?
Bundled together, heads bumping heads,
nine tired lions are ready for bed.

Home is a space that's cozy and warm.
And sleep is a place where they'll come to no harm.

Ten little lions murmur and sigh
beneath the stars and the moon's wide eye,
listening to evening's lullaby.

Ten little lions huddled up tight.
Soon they are sleeping, cuddled by night.